Speak Up, Spike!

Franzeska G. Ewart

Mark Oliver

Go Bananas

Greetings honoured reader.
I am Rama, the brave and
noble prince. This is Sita,
light of my life!

Before you turn
the page, prepare
to be amazed!

The book you hold
in your hand tells of a boy
called Spike and the monsters
he finds in darkness.

Do not be afraid,
gentle reader, Rama and Sita
will read it with you!

For Katherine, Jack, Andrew and Lauren with love
F.G.E.

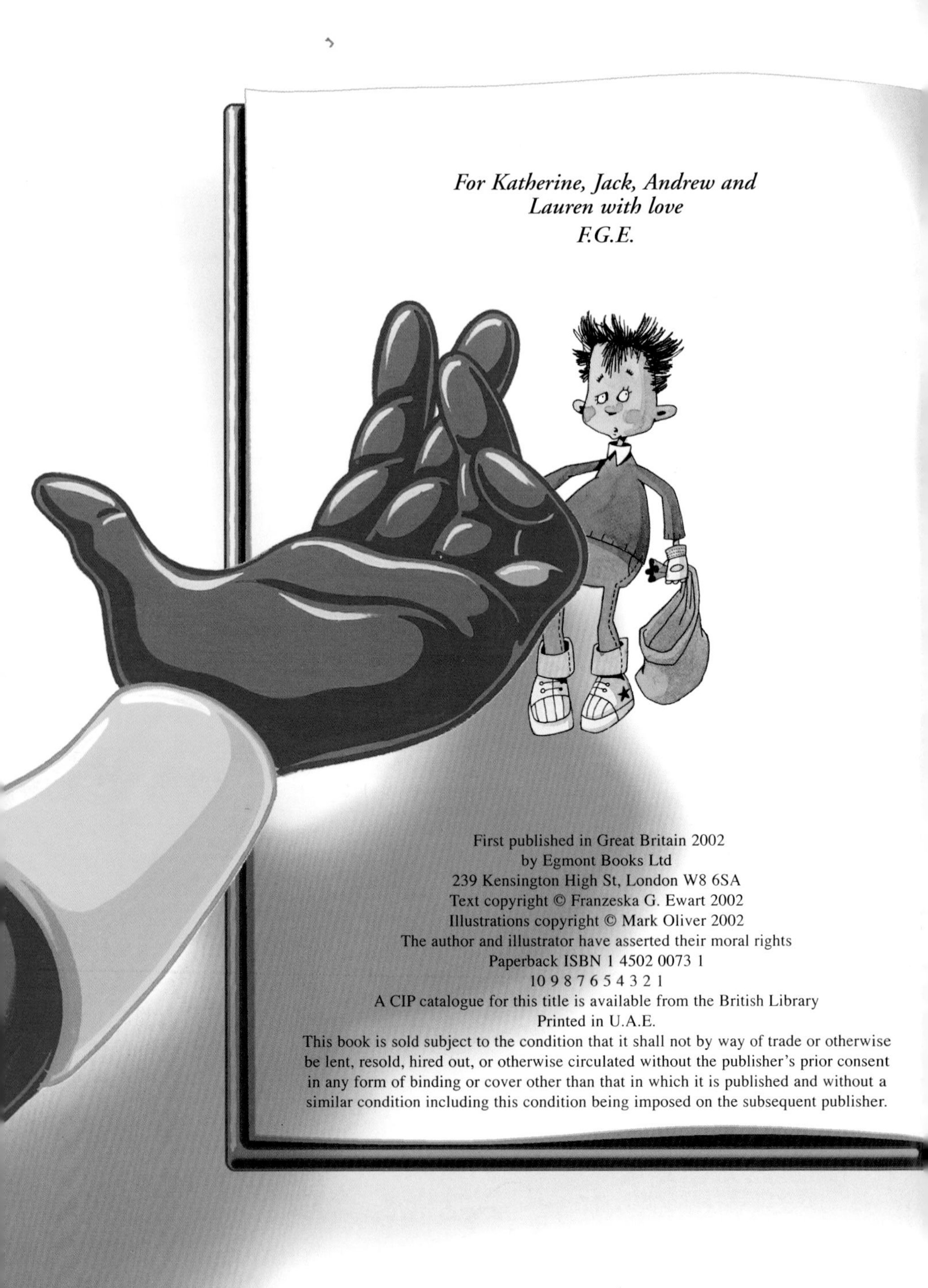

First published in Great Britain 2002
by Egmont Books Ltd
239 Kensington High St, London W8 6SA

Paperback ISBN 1 4502 0073 1
10 9 8 7 6 5 4 3 2 1
A CIP catalogue for this title is available from the British Library
Printed in U.A.E.

Chapter 1

SPIKE WAS A little boy who lived in a big house, full of big brothers, big sisters, and several huge cousins. His dad was big, and his mum was big. Everyone, including the cat, seemed bigger than Spike. And everyone, except Spike, had enormous voices.

When all the big people crowded round Spike and boomed down at him, it made him feel very tiny. The louder the big people shouted, the quieter Spike spoke, so eventually his voice was as tiny as a mouse's squeak. People were always saying,'Speak up, Spike!' But he couldn't.

Night time was worst. Spike was especially scared in the dark, because the dark was full of huge monsters.

When he was younger, Spike's mum had given him a night-light shaped like a toadstool, with a frog on the top. It glowed comfortingly beside his bed. Spike knew he shouldn't really need a night-light now, but he just couldn't get to sleep without it.

It was all right, usually, if he stayed in bed. But if he had to get up to go to the bathroom, those monsters were waiting for him . . . And there was one particular monster that scared Spike more than anything.

No matter how slowly and quietly Spike got up, it would slither out of bed behind him. Then, it would slide along the wall, loom up in front of him, and block the bedroom door.

When Spike reached for the doorknob, the monster's terrible hand would reach for it too, and as soon as the door was open, out it dived into the hall.

Then, something even more awful happened. In the hall the monster grew to twice the size! Its great legs bent and wobbled up the walls, and it was so tall that its huge horny head almost reached the ceiling. By the time Spike reached the bathroom door, his heart was pounding. But even then the monster would not go away.

It bolted into the bathroom, curled itself round and round the toilet roll and clung to the ceiling, watching his every move.

Some nights, Spike made such a noise running back to his bed that it woke his mum and dad. His mum would come in and say, 'What is the matter, Spike?'

Then Spike would cuddle into her warm, comforting nightie and tell her about the monster.

'Oh Spike!' she would say, licking her hand and smoothing his hair down. 'There's no need to be so frightened, there aren't really any monsters!'

Sometimes, his dad came in too.

'Oh Spike!' he would say, giving him a hearty pat on his little back. 'You're afraid of your own shadow! You really should grow out of it.'

When they went away, Spike would curl into the smallest ball he could make and bury his head under the duvet. He wished like anything that he would grow out of it.

Chapter 2

IT WAS DECEMBER, and the days were frosty and bright. Spike was sitting on the classroom floor with the rest of the class, at Mrs Pugh's enormous feet.

Mrs Pugh was the biggest teacher in the world, Spike thought. Even her hair was big. It stood out in huge grey curls, like a lion's mane.

And her voice was so loud you could hear her on the other side of the football pitch, even in a strong gale.

This morning, though, Mrs Pugh was sitting quietly with her enormous teachers' bag on her knees. She leant over it and smiled at them all.

'Who knows what the next festival's going to be?' she asked.

Lots of hands shot up. '*Before* Christmas,' Mrs Pugh added, and lots of hands shot down again.

Aftab's hand stayed where it was.

'Divali, Mrs Pugh,' he said.

As soon as the word was out, Spike felt a tiny shiver of delight shoot up the back of his neck. Divali – the Hindu Festival of Lights! He half-closed his eyes and remembered back to last Divali.

They had made divas, little clay pots just big enough to hold a night-light. Spike's had been the biggest, chunkiest diva of all. It had looked a bit like a potato at first, but when he'd drawn a pattern of green triangles and red hearts round it with felt pen, and painted it all over with clear varnish, Mrs Pugh had said, 'It's stunning, Spike!'

They had set out all the divas in a long wavy line across the classroom floor, Spike remembered, and they had turned off the lights. Spike hadn't liked that bit at all, but then Mrs Pugh had crawled along the floor with a box of matches, and she had lit each diva in turn. It had looked beautiful, like a bright, windy snake. The candle smell and the flickering flames had reminded Spike of his own little toadstool night-light at home, and he had felt much better.

And when Mrs Pugh had set out four trays of wonderfully sticky Indian sweets called burfee and jalebi, he had felt even better.

They had all sat looking at the bright little lights, munching their sweets, and singing their Divali song. It had been simply lovely. He was glad it was Divali time again.

'And this Divali is going to be very, very, very special . . .' Mrs Pugh went on, 'because I've brought some very, very, very special people to show you . . .'

She smiled mysteriously and reached inside her big bag. Out came the strangest person Spike had ever seen. He seemed to be covered in spikes himself!

'This,' Mrs Pugh whispered, 'is a shadow puppet. His name is Rama.'

She held Rama up to the window.

'He's from India, and he's made of leather,' she explained. 'Later, when we turn off the lights, you'll see his shadow!'

Spike's stomach turned over. All the spit in his mouth dried up, so his tongue stuck to his teeth. And, right at the very backs of his eyes, two big tears began to grow.

A great shadow had been cast over wonderful Divali.

Chapter 3

'DOES ANYONE REMEMBER who Rama is?' Mrs Pugh asked, waving the spiky shadow puppet above their heads.

Veronica put up her hand and said, 'He's the brave prince in the Divali story, Mrs Pugh.'

Mrs Pugh beamed at Veronica.

'Spot on!' she said. 'What was the story called?'

'Rama and Sita, Miss,' said Aftab, and Mrs Pugh beamed again.

'Correct!' she smiled.

Mrs Pugh sat back in her big chair, half-closed her eyes, and, in a very soft and mysterious voice, she told them,

'Long, long, long ago in India, there lived a brave and handsome prince called Rama. He was deeply in love with a princess called Sita.'

Mrs Pugh rummaged about in her bag and brought out another shadow puppet. Everyone went 'Oooooooh!' because Princess Sita was very beautiful.

'I want to be her,' Veronica whispered under her breath.

'But the story gets quite sad, doesn't it?' Mrs Pugh went on. 'Because Prince Rama had to go far away, and it was very dangerous. He didn't want Sita to come with him, but she was so deeply in love with him that she did.'

Mrs Pugh closed her eyes. 'A woman's place is at the side of the man she loves . . .' she said dreamily.

Aftab put his hand up and snapped his fingers. Mrs Pugh opened her eyes again.

'The monster came and took Sita away, didn't he, Mrs Pugh?'

'That's right, Aftab,' said Mrs Pugh. 'Prince Rama had gone hunting in the forest, and he told Sita never, ever to step outside the magic circle he had drawn round their house. But the monster, Ravana, came disguised as a deer, didn't he, and tricked poor Sita. She stepped out of the circle, and he changed back and whisked her away to Sri Lanka!'

Spike's mouth got drier and drier as he watched Mrs Pugh's hand slip inside the bag again.

'Can anyone else tell us what Ravana looked like when he wasn't disguised?' she asked, as she slowly pulled out another shadow puppet. It was far bigger than the others.

Gently pushing Aftab's hand back down, Mrs Pugh said, 'Yes, James, you tell us!'

'He had,' James gulped, 'ten heads, and he was vicious.'

'*That's* a good word, James,' Mrs Pugh said. 'Vicious is a very good word for Ravana!'

Spike shuddered.

Vicious, he thought, was a very good word.

'Here we are!' smiled Mrs Pugh, holding the biggest, spikiest shadow puppet up to the light.

Spike covered his eyes with his hands.

'Ravana!' cried Mrs Pugh. 'Who, I am perfectly sure,' she added, looking pointedly at Spike, 'has a very big voice!'

She leaned over and gave Spike a gentle pat on the head with one of Ravana's hands. Spike opened two of his fingers and gulped.

He peered at Ravana through the slits between his fingers.

Mrs Pugh climbed carefully over everyone's heads till she stood at her desk. There was a wooden picture frame stuck to the edge of the desk, and Mrs Pugh began to stretch a cotton sheet over it.

As she did, she explained,

'Now, for there to be a shadow, there needs to be light. And light comes from . . .'

She looked over the picture frame, and raised her eyebrows, which meant she was asking a question.

'Sun!' shouted Aftab.

'Good, Aftab,' said Mrs Pugh. 'But today we need a smaller light, so you may pull down the blinds. Where else does light come from?'

'An electric light!' shouted Veronica.

'Splendid,' said Mrs Pugh. 'Inside this projector is an electric light! When I turn the projector on the light will shine on to the screen. But to see it we'll need to turn the classroom lights off!'

Spike watched in horror as she strode over to the light switches, and he gave a little gasp as she flicked them off.

The classroom was plunged into inky darkness. Spike felt his fingernails dig into the skin on the sides of his knees.

'Now, just you wait and see what happens next!' Mrs Pugh's big voice thundered out above Spike's head.

'Ready?'

There was a soft 'click', and the sheet lit up into a bright rectangle of light.

'See?' said Mrs Pugh. 'We've got our own magic little world now.

She disappeared behind the screen and then, suddenly, her great big shadow head filled the whole rectangle, with a jungle of gigantic curls.

'And here comes . . . Ravana!' she announced importantly.

Spike nearly jumped right off the floor as Mrs Pugh's head was replaced by a terrible shadow monster. It was bigger, and jaggier, and scarier, than anything he had met in the bathroom. It had ten huge heads!

'Ravana's about, so you'd better watch out!' Mrs Pugh boomed, and everyone clung together and pretended to be terrified.

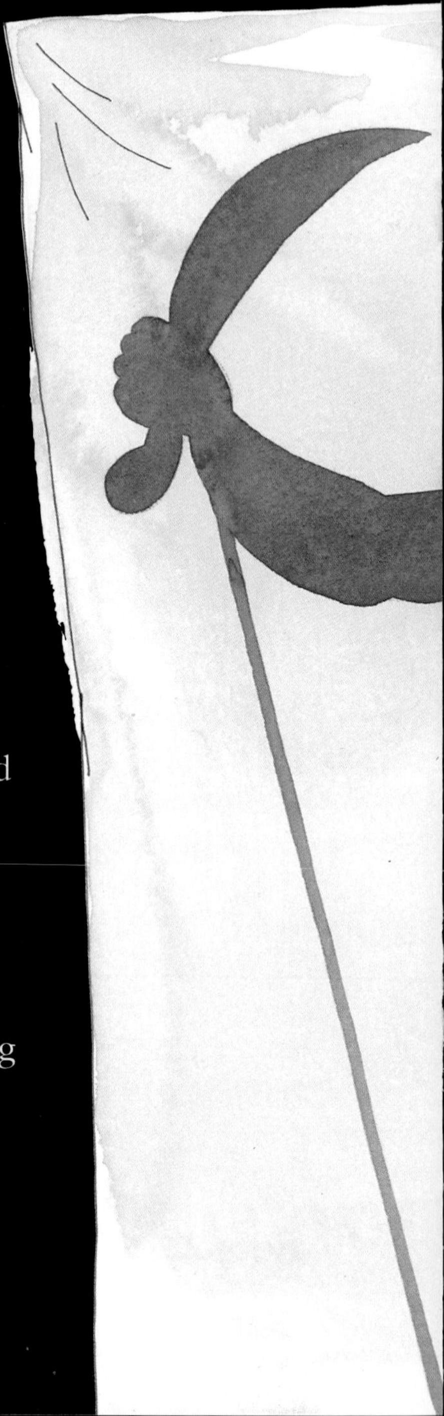

'And that,' she added, popping her head above the screen, 'is how *you* are going to have to do it tomorrow. Because *you* are going to act out the Divali story yourselves.'

Everyone, except Spike, gasped in delight and said, 'Cool!'

'I hope I get to be Rama, the brave prince,' said Aftab wistfully.

'I hope I get to be Sita, the beautiful princess,' sighed Veronica. 'A woman's place is by the side of the man she loves,' she added, looking over at Aftab.

Spike said nothing. He was dashed sure he wasn't going to *be* anyone.

Chapter 4

SPIKE THOUGHT ABOUT shadows all night long, especially when he went to the bathroom. He looked up at the shadow monster, stretching up behind the toilet, and he felt it looking back down at him.

He thought about Ravana, the vicious ten-headed monster, and his hugely scary shadow. He thought about Mrs Pugh, tapping him gently on the head with one of Ravana's hands. And he remembered how, when Mrs Pugh had turned the light back on, Ravana's shadow had simply vanished!

Actually, when you really saw Ravana, he wasn't that big.

Okay, he had ten heads, but none of them were really all that scary.

He was just a leather puppet, after all. He was even smaller than Spike.

When Spike had flushed the toilet and closed the bathroom door behind him, he tiptoed slowly and quietly back to bed. Then, he lifted the duvet and peered into the darkness. You couldn't see anything, he thought. It was one great big shadow in there.

He curled up in a ball and hugged his knees, and as he did, he wondered whether his shadow was lying beside him hugging its knees too, safe inside their blanket of darkness.

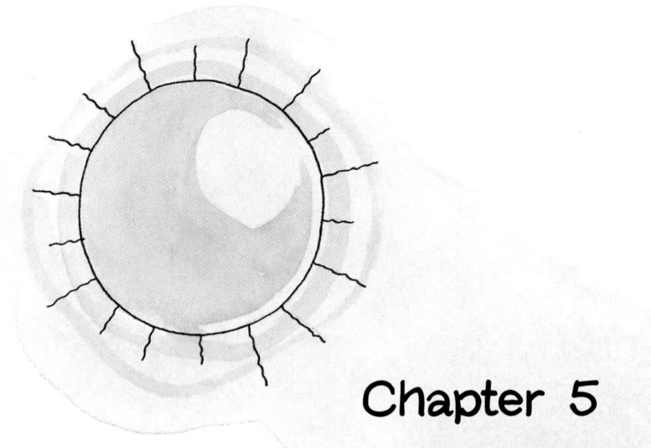

Chapter 5

EARLY NEXT MORNING, Spike was in the playground with a bin-bag, picking up litter. Although it was very cold, the sun shone brightly.

Spike collected litter to earn 'Sunshine Points', which were special stickers you got if you did a Good Thing. The class with the most 'Sunshine Points' got a special 'Sunshine Party'. It was always a wonderful treat.

The next 'Sunshine Party' would be a special Divali one, so there would be mountains of burfee and jalebi, like last year, only far, far, far more.

Primary Three had never won a 'Sunshine Party'. They were the only class in the whole school that hadn't, and Spike was sure it made Mrs Pugh feel really bad.

As he collected, he wondered what was going to happen today when they did their Divali shadow puppet play. His stomach gave a little lurch and his mouth went dry just thinking about it.

Suddenly, Spike gasped. There was a monster in the playground with him. It had spiky hair, just like his, and it had its own, almost-empty bin-bag! It was huge!

Very carefully, Spike lifted one leg so that it stuck right out to the side. The shadow monster stuck its big leg out too. Spike put his leg down again and slowly, wobbling a great deal, he stuck out the other one. It looked really funny. He wiggled his foot about.

The huge shadow foot wiggled too. He kept on doing it, over and over and over again. And then the shadow monster disappeared, drowned in a great black sea. Spike felt a big hand on his shoulder and, looking down, he saw Mrs Pugh's enormous feet planted one on either side of his own.

'What are you doing, Spike? The bell's long gone!' Mrs Pugh said angrily.

'I'm playing with my shadow,' Spike whispered.

'Speak up, Spike!' Mrs Pugh shouted.

'I'm playing with my shadow,' Spike repeated. Then he turned round and, in a voice he had never heard before, he said,

'I don't think I'm scared of my shadow any more.'

'Good!' said Mrs Pugh, twisting Spike round and marching him in the direction of the door. Spike squinted up at her. She had a very funny look on her face, he thought. She was up to something.

When they reached the classroom door, Mrs Pugh stopped and crouched down so that she was level with Spike. Spike blinked several times. He had never been this close to a teacher before.

'Know how many 'Sunshine Points' we need to win the 'Sunshine Party', Spike?' Mrs Pugh said.

Spike shook his head.

'Ten,' said Mrs Pugh.

Spike blinked again. Mrs Pugh's nose was so close he could see his face reflected in her glasses. He did not speak.

'Know how someone could earn us those ten 'Sunshine Points', Spike?' Mrs Pugh whispered, and as she did, she winked.

Spike wrinkled his little brow. He bit his lip.

'How, Mrs Pugh?' he asked.

'You'll see,' Mrs Pugh answered, and pushed him gently through the door.

Chapter 6

EVERYONE STARED AT Spike, who sat down on the floor and tried to look tiny. Veronica was glaring out from behind the shadow screen, holding the Sita puppet.

'All right, Veronica and Aftab,' said Mrs Pugh briskly. 'Let's hear your lines again. Then Ravana will make his entrance.'

She turned off the lights and the screen glowed. There was a great deal of scuffling, and for a moment all that was seen was the shadow of Veronica's head. Then Aftab's appeared, and the two shadows frowned at one another.

'Sit down, for goodness sake!' Mrs Pugh growled. 'We don't want to see you. We want to see Rama and Sita!'

At last the shadowy Veronica and Aftab disappeared, and everyone gasped as Rama and Sita stood before them. The puppets wobbled, and Veronica cleared her throat.

'Oh Rama!' she said, in a very high voice. 'Do not leave me! I am so afraid!'

There was silence and both puppets slithered off the screen.

'It's you!' Veronica hissed. 'Do not be afraid my darling . . .'

Aftab's head popped out. His face was very red.

'Miss, do I have to call her *my darling?*' he said. 'Can I not just call her *Sita*?'

Mrs Pugh sighed. 'You are deeply in love with her, Aftab, like it or not,' she said wearily.

As she spoke, she pulled Spike to his feet. Spike felt Ravana's rods pressed into his hands, and he wobbled under the weight of the big shadow puppet.

'Do not be afraid . . . my darling!' Aftab's voice floated through the darkness. 'Stay in the magic circle and you will . . . you will . . .'

'You will come to no harm!' shouted Mrs Pugh. She steered Spike into the pool of light and pushed him down.

'Come on,' she whispered in his ear. 'Say, *Ravana's about, so you'd better watch out!*'

Spike swallowed hard and stuck the shadow puppet into the overhead projector's beam. Ravana's shadow filled the screen. Spike gazed dizzily up at him. He pulled the puppet towards him so that its shadow grew even bigger.

He had never seen anything so huge. His heart pounded and his tongue stuck to the roof of his mouth.

Mrs Pugh knelt down beside him. She held one of the rods for him, and together they made Ravana move out and in. He grew bigger, then smaller, then bigger again.

'Come on, Spike,' Mrs Pugh whispered, giving him a nudge. 'There's ten 'Sunshine Points' in it if you do!'

Spike took a deep breath. He thought how pleased Mrs Pugh would be if they won a 'Sunshine Party' at last. But his mouth was so dry his tongue just wouldn't move.

He thought about great mountains of burfee and jalebi. He thought about pink burfee, and green burfee, and burfee with nuts in . . . Spike licked his lips. Then he looked up at the great big shadow monster in his hands and he shouted, 'Ravana's about, so you'd better watch out!'

'Great, but do speak up, Spike,' whispered Mrs Pugh gently. 'Do it really viciously. *You're* the big monster now!'

This time, when Spike did his lines, it felt like the whole school would come crashing down on top of him.

'RAVANA'S ABOUT,' he boomed, 'SO YOU'D BETTER WATCH OUT!'

His voice was so loud, and so ferocious, that Veronica stepped backwards into Aftab, and they both landed on the floor in a mass of rods and leather.

'Well done, Spike!' said Mrs Pugh. She disentangled Veronica and Aftab from Rama and Sita, dusted them all down, and then switched the classroom lights back on.

'A magnificent performance,' she beamed, pulling Spike out from behind the screen and holding Ravana high above his head. 'And well worth ten 'Sunshine Points', I think!'

Spike crawled back into the crowd of children on the floor. Everyone patted him on the back and told him how scary he'd been.

'You were truly vicious, Spike,' said Veronica admiringly.

'You've won us our first 'Sunshine Party', Spike,' Aftab said. 'It'll be the best Divali ever!'

But Spike wasn't listening. He was thinking about how big he'd made Ravana's shadow grow.

He was thinking about how scary he had made Ravana be.

And, most of all, he was thinking about the big, deep voice he'd never known he had. It could scare even the biggest monster away!

Spike smiled happily. It was going to be the best Divali ever, without a shadow of a doubt.

What a hero Spike is – as brave as a prince! He defeated his fears just as I defeated the monster, Ravana!

After Rama saved me from Ravana, people lit our way home through the darkness with lamps.

Ever since, at the same time of year, Hindu people have celebrated Rama's victory. This is the joyous festival called Divali!

Find a torch and turn off the light in your room, so it's very dark! Then turn on your torch and point it at the wall. What you see is a light beam! Light travels in a straight line, until something gets in its way, like a wall.

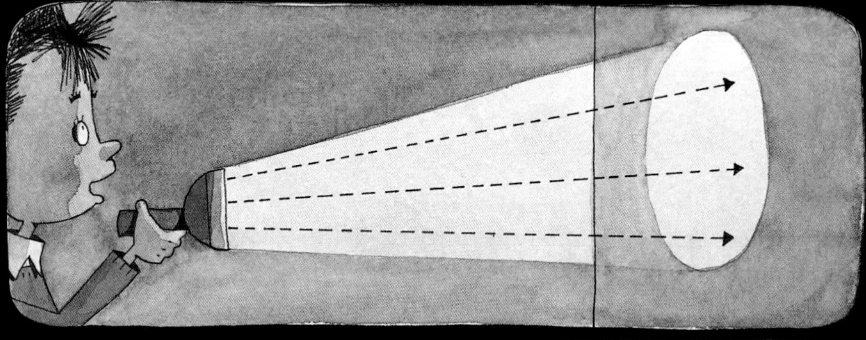

Put your hand over the light, so it covers the beam. What happens?

A thing that blocks light is described as opaque.

Try putting your hand in the light's beam. What happens now?

Some of the light is blocked by my hand and a shadow is formed!

Move your hand around. What does your shadow do?
Look what happens if I move my hand closer to the torch.
My shadow gets bigger!

This is because more light is blocked when my hand is close to the torch than when it is further away.

A long time ago, a scientist was climbing the Brocken Mountain in Germany. Suddenly, he became aware of a huge, scary figure in front of him in the clouds. It was far bigger than the monster in my bathroom. It was even bigger than Ravana! But it was only his shadow!

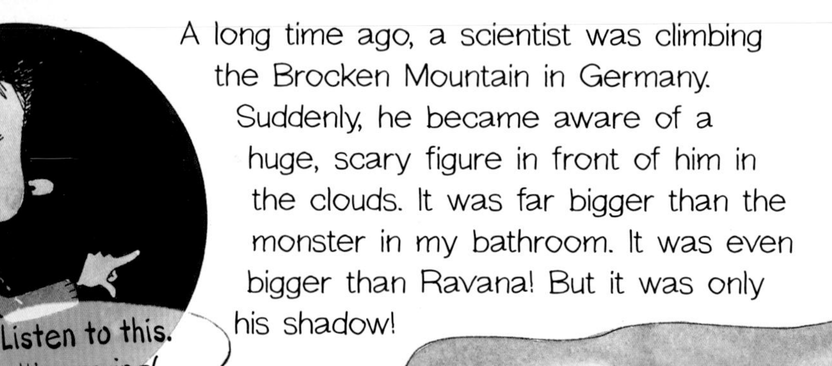

Just as the torch cast a shadow of my hand against the wall, the sun cast a shadow of the climber on the passing clouds.

What you will need:

1 big sheet of black sugar paper or thin card
1 pencil or pen
1 pair of scissors
1 plant stick or knitting needle
Some sticky tape
1 good, strong torch
1 space on a light coloured wall
1 hole puncher
1 dark night

Make your own Spooky Shadow Puppet!

1 Think of a scary figure! Now draw it on your page. Remember it needs to be big! Bigger than this book when it's open. It could look like these:

I'm not scared!

2 Carefully cut out your figure and stick the plant stick to the back, like this:

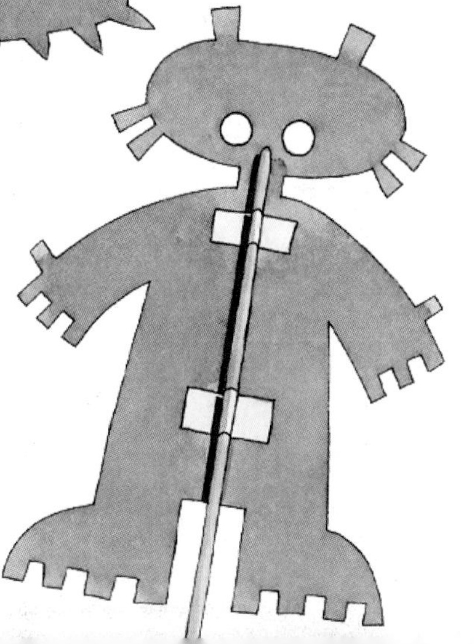

3 You can use the hole puncher to make eyes.

4 Wait until night fall. Close the curtains, draw the blinds and turn the lights off!

5 Turn your torch on and point it at the wall. A circle of light should appear. What happens if you move your torch further away from the wall? That's right, the circle grows! Once the light is the size of a dustbin lid or bigger, rest your torch on a chair.

6 Now put your puppet in the light beam. See how its shadow grows and shrinks as you move the puppet in and out?

7 Give your monster a voice. What scary things might he say?